Leila at the Library
and the Letter L

Alphabet Friends

by Cynthia Klingel and Robert B. Noyed

The Child's World®

The Child's World®

Published in the United States of America
by The Child's World®
P.O. Box 326
Chanhassen, MN 55317-0326
800-599-READ
www.childsworld.com

The Child's World®: Mary Berendes, Publishing Director

Editorial Directions, Inc.: E. Russell Primm, Editorial
Director; Emily Dolbear, Line Editor; Ruth Martin,
Editorial Assistant; Linda S. Koutris, Photo Researcher
and Selector

Photographs ©: Stockbyte/Picture Quest: Cover & 9,
21; Mark Gamba/Corbis: 10; Corbis: 13, 17, 18; Joe
McDonald/Corbis: 14.

Library of Congress Cataloging-in-Publication Data
Klingel, Cynthia Fitterer.
  Leila at the library and the letter L / by Cynthia
Klingel and Robert B. Noyed.
    p. cm. — (Alphabet readers)
Summary: A simple story about a girl named Leila and
what she learns at the library introduce the letter "l".
  ISBN 1-59296-102-9 (Library Bound : alk. paper)
  [1. Libraries—Fiction. 2. Alphabet.] I. Noyed, Robert B.
II. Title. III. Series.
  PZ7.K6798Ld 2003
  [E]—dc21   2003006608

Note to parents and educators:

The first skill children acquire before becoming successful readers is individual letter recognition. The Alphabet Friends series has been created with the needs of young learners in mind. Each engaging book begins by showing the difference between the capital letter and the lowercase letter. In each of the books on the vowels and the consonants c and g, children are introduced to the different sounds that the letter can make. Finally, children see that the letters can be found at the beginning of a word, in the middle of a word, and in most cases, at the end of a word.

Following the introduction, children meet their Alphabet Friends. The friend in each story encounters many words that include the featured letter of that book. Each noun that begins with the title letter is highlighted in red with the initial letter of the word in bold. Above the word is a rebus drawing that establishes a strong picture cue.

At the end of each book, we have included three words lists. Can your young learners find all the words in each book with the title letter in them?

Let's learn about the letter **L.**

The letter **L** can look like this: **L.**

The letter **L** can also look like this: **I.**

The letter **l** can be at the

beginning of a word, like lamp.

lamp

The letter **l** can be in the

middle of a word, like island.

is**l**and

The letter **l** can be at the

end of a word, like baseball.

baseba**l**

Leila loves to go to the library. She

learns many things at the library.

She loves to look at books.

Leila finds a place to sit in the library.

It is by a lamp. Sitting by the lamp will

help her see the books.

Leila learns about lions in a library book.

Lions have long hair around their face.

This long hair is called a mane.

Leila learns about leopards in a library

book. Leopards have a lot of spots.

Leopards and lions are big cats.

Leila learns about lambs in a library

book. Lambs live on farms. Leila learns

that lambs are little sheep.

Leila learns about **ll**amas in a **l**ibrary

book. **Ll**amas live in the hills. **Ll**amas

are related to camels.

Leila is learning many things at the library.

It is time for Leila to leave. She will return

later to look at more books.

Fun Facts

Leopards are large members of the cat family. Most leopards are tan-colored and covered with many black spots. Some leopards, like the ones that live in forests, are so dark that their spots are hard to see. They look completely black. Black leopards are often called panthers.

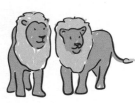

Unlike most cats, lions like to live in groups. A group of lions that live together is called a pride. Each pride stays within a particular area of land. Lions do not let animals outside their pride hunt in their territory. They scare intruders away with their powerful roar. A lion's roar can be heard by humans more than 5 miles (8 kilometers) away!

A llama looks like a small camel without its hump. Llamas are used as pack animals in the Andes Mountains in South America. Pack animals are animals that carry packages, but not people. If llamas feel they've worked too hard, they will lie down and refuse to get up. They might also spit at their driver!

To Read More

About the Letter L

Flanagan, Alice K. *Left: The Sound of L.* Chanhassen, Minn.: The Child's World, 2000.

About Leopards

Fontes, Justine Korman, Ron Fontes, and Keiko Motoyama (illustrator). *How the Leopard Got Its Spots: Three Tales from around the World.* New York: Golden Books, 1999.

Middleton, Don. *Leopards.* New York: PowerKids Press, 1999.

About Lions

Kendell, Patricia. *Lions.* Austin, Tex.: Raintree Steck-Vaughn, 2002.

Schneider, Antonie, and Cristina Kadmon (illustrator). *Luke the Lionhearted.* New York: North-South Books, 1998.

About Llamas

Frisch, Aaron. *Llamas.* Mankato, Minn.: Creative Education, 2002.

Voss, Gisela, and Melissa Sweet. *Llama in Pajamas.* Boston: Museum of Fine Arts, 1994.

Words with L

Words with L at the Beginning
lambs
lamp
later
learn
learning
learns
leave
Leila
leopards
let's
letter
library
like
lions
little
live
llamas
long
look
lot
loves

Words with L in the Middle
baseball
called
camels
help
hills
island
Leila
place
related
well
will

Words with L at the End
baseball
well
will

About the Authors

Cynthia Klingel has worked as a high school English teacher and an elementary teacher. She is currently the curriculum director for a Minnesota school district. Cynthia Klingel lives with her family in Mankato, Minnesota.

Robert B. Noyed started his career as a newspaper reporter. Since then, he has worked in communications and public relations for a Minnesota school district for more than fourteen years. Robert B. Noyed lives with his family in Brooklyn Center, Minnesota.